Vera Rosenberry

Vera's Baby Sister

Henry Holt and Company

New York

A new baby had arrived at Vera's house.
The baby made a lot of noise.

Friends and family visited.

They all brought presents for the baby. They smiled.
They cooed. They chattered and clattered.

There was no peace for Vera.

She couldn't sleep at night.

She couldn't read.

She couldn't draw.

If she went into the bathroom and locked the door—
bang! bang!—someone needed to come in.

Vera looked down at baby Ruthie. She did not think she was cute. Ruthie looked like an old prune. Vera secretly made her ugliest face at the baby.

"I wish you could take that baby back to the hospital," she announced. "I hate her!" But no one seemed to be listening to Vera.

Grandfather was making soup in the
kitchen when Vera dragged herself in.
"That baby fills up the whole house,"
Vera said. "It used to be nice here,
but now there is no room for me."

Grandfather looked at Vera. He saw how sad she was.

"Come outside with me," he said. "I know something that may help you feel better."

Grandfather was holding a few ordinary dried beans, the kind used to make soup.

It was a beautiful spring day, with fluffy clouds in a soft blue sky.

"Come on," Grandfather said. "I have a plan."

Together, they dug a neat square of earth, breaking up the grass and turning over the soil. It was hard work and took a long time.

"Now," said Grandfather, "we need a few big sticks."
"I know where we can find some," said Vera. "By my school."
They soon found eight good sticks in the woods.

Carrying the sticks between them, they pretended to be a train, all the way home.

choo choo choooo!!!

Vera heard the baby crying as they passed her bedroom window. How could anyone like that loud, smelly thing? *"WAA, WAA, WAAA!"*

Grandfather poked the eight sticks
into the ground and made a circle.

"We'll tie them together at the top
with string," he explained.

"It looks like a tent," said Vera.

Grandfather nodded. "This is the most important part. Help me plant these beans all around the sticks. Then we shall see what happens."

After they buried the beans, Vera ran inside. She brought out her special stool and put it in the tent.

Grandfather hung a bird feeder on the longest stick, and he filled it with sunflower seeds. He gave the bag of seeds to Vera so she could keep the feeder full.

Vera sat on her stool and watched birds come and go. She liked the way the sun shone on the sticks and made interesting shadows. Most of all, she liked the peace and quiet. She read her library books and forgot about the horrible baby.

One rainy day, Vera noticed sturdy green shoots
poking up all around the circle of sticks. She was very
careful not to crush them.

Soon, the shoots grew tall. They had lovely broad leaves and
twisty ends that wrapped themselves around the sticks, higher
and higher.

Before long, it was hot summer. Vines and large leaves covered the sticks. They made a shady, secret house around Vera as she sat on her stool inside.

"This is the most beautiful place in the world. And it is all mine. No babies in here," Vera whispered to the birds and caterpillars and butterflies and ladybugs, who were also enjoying the tent.

In time, the bean vines made flowers that turned into green beans. Vera picked them and brought the beans to her mother to cook.

Grandfather came to visit. "Delicious!" he exclaimed, when he ate the beans. "I see you have taken care of the bean tent, Vera, and it has grown up well."

Vera smiled proudly.

In the autumn, as it grew cooler, the bean vines dried up. Vera gathered seeds from the remaining pods and held them in her hand— warm, smooth, brown seeds. Each one held so much life inside it!

She wrote "Vera's Bean Tent" on
an envelope with a green crayon and
slipped in her seeds.

Vera glanced down at her baby sister, who was sleeping in a carriage out in the sunshine.

Ruthie didn't look so ugly anymore, especially
when she was asleep. Her face was smooth and rosy.
Vera realized she didn't cry so much lately either.

Ruthie opened her big, round eyes and stretched
her chubby arms up to Vera.

That made Vera laugh. Ruthie laughed, too.
"Maybe, if you are a GOOD little sister,"
Vera said, "I will make a special bean tent
next year for you."

To Ruth

Henry Holt and Company, LLC
Publishers since 1866
115 West 18th Street
New York, New York 10011
www.henryholt.com

Henry Holt is a registered trademark of Henry Holt and Company, LLC
Copyright © 2005 by Vera Rosenberry
All rights reserved.
Distributed in Canada by H. B. Fenn and Company Ltd.

Library of Congress Cataloging-in-Publication Data
Rosenberry, Vera.
Vera's baby sister / Vera Rosenberry.—1st ed.
p.   cm.
Summary: The arrival of Vera's new baby sister makes her feel displaced,
so her grandfather helps create a special spot, just for her.
ISBN-13: 978-0-8050-7126-9
ISBN-10: 0-8050-7126-1
[1. Sibling rivalry—Fiction. 2. Babies—Fiction. 3. Grandfathers—Fiction.] I. Title.
PZ7.R719155Vde 2005
[E]—dc22
2004009202

First Edition—2005 / Designed by Amy Manzo Toth
Printed in the United States of America on acid-free paper. ∞

1   3   5   7   9   10   8   6   4   2

The artist used gouache on Lanaquarelle paper to create the illustrations for this book.